LITTLE SPUD

You may not be like all the other little dragons but you can still shine.

Written ... rie Stell

D1633775

3411404005180 6

Printed in the United Kingdom
First Printing, 2021
ISBN: Print (Soft Cover):
978-1-8383723-4-7

Published by Purple Parrot Publishing
www.purpleparrotpublishing.co.uk

DEDICATION

'Little Spud' is dedicated to my mum, Bernie, for encouraging me and having faith in me to do this.

To my family, friends and more who believed in me so much that they supported me.

To the 'Purple Parrot', Vivienne, who has worked wonders and made this a reality.

And last but definitely not least, to my brother Christopher, without whom, none of this would exist.

"In a world full of darkness, he is the light."

Marie x

10% of sales of the book will be donated to the National Autistic Society, a registered charity in England and Wales (269425) and in Scotland (SC039427).

Have you ever felt
like you don't belong?

That you're not good enough
and that all you do is wrong?

Not fast enough at running
or cannot catch a ball?

Your feet don't work too well
and you often have a fall?

Or maybe you can't see or hear,
do you struggle to understand?

Confused by what folks say and mean,
or locked in your own land?

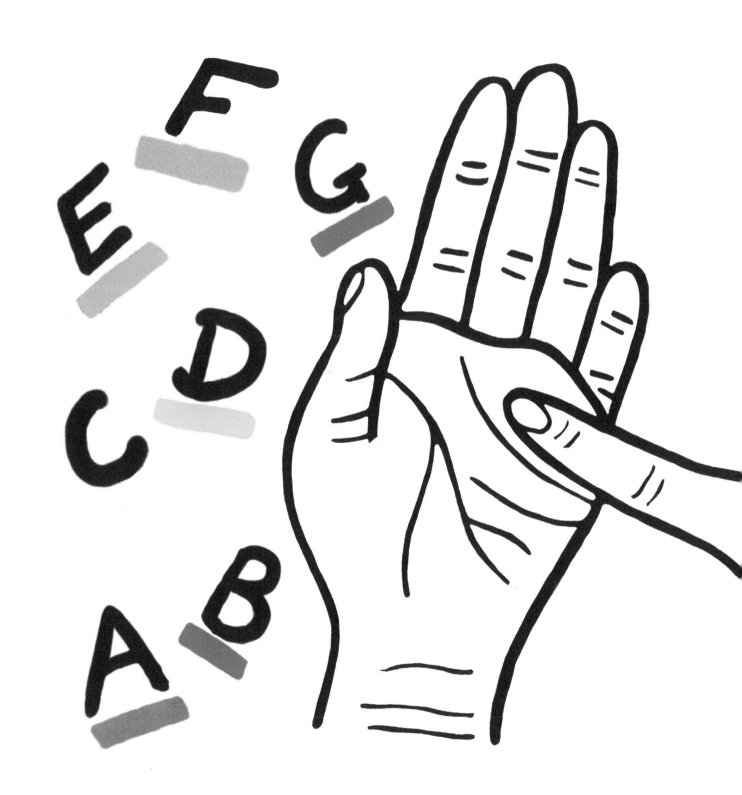

No two dragons are the same,
all precious and unique,

You're entitled to be heard,
even if you cannot speak.

Don't listen if they tell you
that you're not good enough.

Your time to shine will come,
Like a diamond in the rough.

You may not quite believe me
but what I say is true.

Magic is alive
and it lives inside of you!

Well, if you're having doubts
about what you can achieve,
sit back and read my story
and in yourself you will believe.

Let me introduce myself,
my name is Little Spud.
My sister wrote this story,
in the hope of doing good.

Not quite like other dragons,
it took time to learn to fly.
I never could breathe fire,
but everyday I try.

Change is hard to cope with,
I don't go out alone.

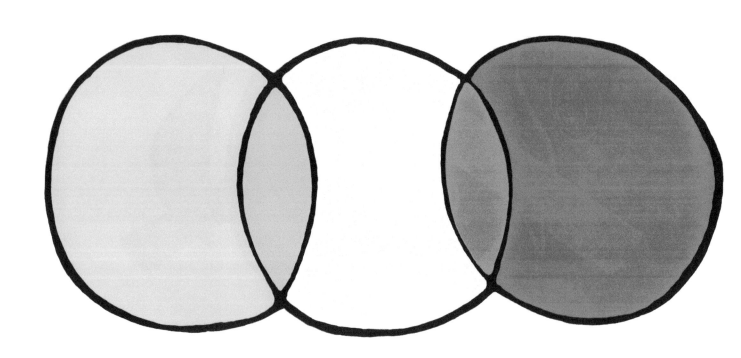

Autistic Spectrum

I'm on the Autistic Spectrum
and have a loving family home.

All are = equal

It's hard to make new friends
but I am a friendly guy.
Yet some dragons can be hurtful,
nasty, cruel and sly.

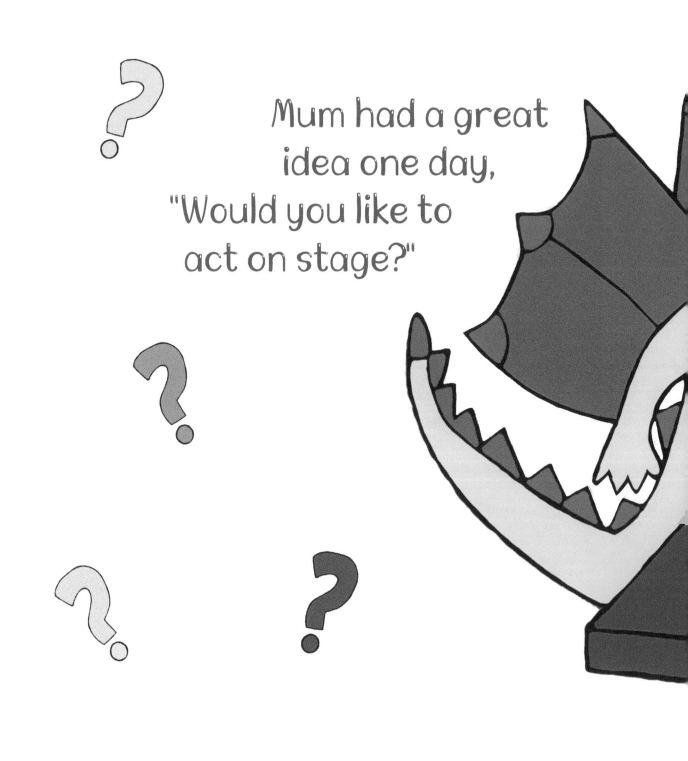

Mum had a great
idea one day,
"Would you like to
act on stage?"

So I joined a local
drama group,
and my life, it
turned a page.

I enjoyed backstage and acting;
learning, having fun.
I felt at ease and happy,
making friends with everyone.

My acting became much better
but some 'friends' began to change
their attitudes towards me
and I found it very strange.

"Quiet! Shut up! Stop it!
Your opinion doesn't count!
Needed help so you don't deserve credit!"
The insults began to mount.

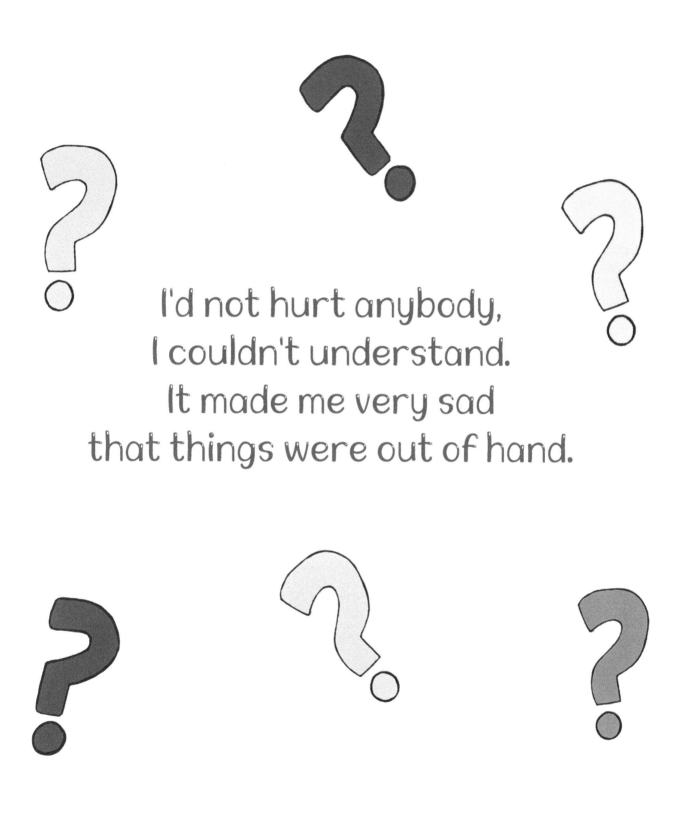

I'd not hurt anybody,
I couldn't understand.
It made me very sad
that things were out of hand.

My Mum was there to help me
as I tried hard not to cry.
"Don't worry my brave
young dragon,
there are those
that can be sly."

"It could be that they're jealous of how much you've improved. Don't try to understand them, stay strong and don't be moved."

It was tough but it paid off,
as I went and tried my best.
A talent agent saw me act,
"You must come for your screen test."

I was happy but so nervous,
I gave it everything I had.

The agents smiled as they approached me and I knew it wasn't bad.

I'd proved the bullies wrong, I was on the silver screen!

The first dragon in the leading role, the World had ever seen.

My family are so proud of me
and dreams they can come true.
Stay strong and do your best,
and your magic will shine through.

The moral of this story is
no matter who you are,
anyone who wants to
can be the brightest star.

For Spud x